Sshaboom!

Sshaboom!

BY BRIAN MANGAS · ILLUSTRATED BY KATY BRATUN

SIMON & SCHUSTER BOOKS FOR YOUNG READERS
Published by Simon & Schuster
New York • London • Toronto • Sydney • Tokyo • Singapore

SIMON & SCHUSTER BOOKS FOR YOUNG READERS
Simon & Schuster Building, Rockefeller Center, 1230 Avenue of the Americas
New York, New York 10020. Text copyright © 1993 by Brian Mangas. Illustrations
copyright © 1993 by Katy Bratun. All rights reserved including the right of
reproduction in whole or in part in any form. SIMON & SCHUSTER BOOKS FOR
YOUNG READERS is a trademark of Simon & Schuster. Designed by David Neuhaus.
The text for this book was set in 18 pt. Garamond #3. The illustrations were
done in colored pencil.
Manufactured in the United States of America   10   9   8   7   6   5   4   3   2   1

Library of Congress Cataloging-in-Publication Data
Mangas, Brian. Sshaboom!/by Brian Mangas; illustrated by Katy Bratun.
Summary: A plumbing problem creates a small flood in the Rabbit house that
almost washes all the bunnies away.   [1. Rabbits—Fiction.   2. Floods—Fiction.]
I. Bratun, Katy, ill.   II. Title.
PZ7.M312644Sh   1992   [E]—dc20   CIP   91-24764
ISBN 0-671-75538-2

For my mother, Eileen   —BM

For my parents, Alma and Rudy   —KB

Father MacBunny tasted the carrot stew. "It's almost done," he said.

Betsy MacBunny set the table. She wanted to
have everything ready before Mother came home.

Betsy stepped in a puddle of water. "Why is the floor all wet?" she asked.

"There must be a leak," Father MacBunny said. Water was dripping out of the cabinet under the sink.

Father MacBunny opened the cabinet door.

Ssha!

The pipe was leaking.

"It's only a small leak," Father MacBunny said. "I'll fix it."

Father MacBunny crawled under the sink. He banged on the pipes. He tightened the connections.

But he didn't stop the leak.

Betsy went to get a towel for Father.
From the next room she heard a loud. . .

ssha. . .   ssha. . .

ssha...

B-O-O-M!

"Oh, no!" Father MacBunny cried.
"It's a flood."
Water poured out of the kitchen and
into the dining room.

Betsy ran upstairs. Father MacBunny
swam into the living room.
The water got deeper.

Then Mother and Billy came home.

Mother MacBunny was carrying grocery bags and couldn't get out her key.

Billy knocked on the door and rang the bell. No one answered.

"That's odd," Mother MacBunny said. "I hear noises in there. They must be home."

Mother MacBunny put down her packages and found her key.

When she opened the door, a wave lifted her and Billy and washed them across the lawn.

Mrs. O'Hare from next door saw what happened. She went outside to help Mother MacBunny and Billy. "Do you need some help?" she asked.

"I think we need a plumber," Mother MacBunny said.

Mrs. O'Hare called a plumber.

When the plumber got there, he turned off all the water in the house. "This job will take a few days," he said. "You bunnies had better go to a hotel."

The bunnies went to a hotel to wait
for their house to be fixed.

The hotel manager said they could
use the swimming pool.

"No, thank you," they said. "We
don't want to swim today."

After the bunnies went to their room, the hotel manager turned to the bellhop. "I wonder why they don't want to swim," he said. "It's such a nice day."